BOATS

by Anne Rockwell

E. P. Dutton • New York

Library of Congress number 82-2420
ISBN 0-525-44219-7
Published in the United States by E. P. Dutton,
2 Park Avenue, New York, N.Y. 10016
a division of NAL Penguin Inc.
Published simultaneously in Canada by
Fitzhenry & Whiteside Limited, Toronto
Editor: Ann Durell   Designer: Isabel Warren-Lynch
Printed in Hong Kong by South China Printing Co.
First Unicorn Edition 1985   COBE
10 9 8 7 6 5 4 3

Boats float.

They float on quiet ponds,

and busy rivers,

and the wide, blue sea.

Some boats are big.

Some boats are small.

Some boats go fast.

Some boats go slow.

What makes a boat go?
Oars and paddles make some boats go.

Wind-filled sails make others go.

Motors and engines make some boats go,

and barges are pulled or pushed by tugs.

There are boats for work

and boats for play.

On all the busy waters of our world,

there are boats.